The Whole Truth

Written by Joanna Nadin

Illustrated by Volker Beisler

Chapter 1
Nothing But Lies

Marcie Hopkins was eight years old. She had brown hair, a nose like a button, and knew her times tables up to six. She was a completely ordinary girl, a fact that annoyed her, a lot. Especially because of her twin brother, Armitage.

Armitage, being a twin, was also eight years old. He also had brown hair, a nose like a button, and knew his times tables up to six. But this boy was far from ordinary, because of one teeny-tiny difference.

Armitage Hopkins told lies. Not just small ones like, "It wasn't me who ate the last raspberry ripple wafer. Honestly it wasn't!" No, Armitage told big, hairy whoppers. Worst of all, no one seemed to care, except Marcie.

If Marcie complained, "Mum, Armitage is picking his nose at the table!" Armitage would say, "But I'm not picking my nose. I'm checking that my Sonic Tracker is still safely inside my left nostril." And Mum would say, "That's nice, dear."

Barry liked this programme.

Or, if Armitage told Granny that his ink pen was actually a device that could track and change the thoughts of wicked villains, she would say, "Ooh, really? That's just like my cat, Barry. He can change the channel on the television just by miaowing." Which wasn't true either, it was just that Granny's television was on the blink.

Take last Monday, for example. First, Armitage lied to Mum about why his trousers were covered in sticky green gloop.

"Lord Zarg summoned me to his headquarters, but on the way back I got lost in the Forest of Eternal Gloom and fell into the Swamp of Certain Death. It was lucky I had my Jet-Action Rocket Boots on, and I managed to zoom out before I got sucked into the murky lair of the Mud Monster."

Next, he lied to Mr Hegarty, the headmaster, about why he hadn't done his maths homework.

"Oh, I did do it, sir. It's just that it accidentally got caught in the stream of flames from my Jet-Action Rocket Boots and got completely zapped in the massive heat."

Then, he lied to Mrs Bottomley, the dinner lady, about why he didn't want 'Fish Surprise' for lunch.

"Juju Jack, the world's most menacing monkey, swore to Lord Zarg that he would get his own back for spoiling his plan to rule the world (again), by poisoning all food beginning with the letter 'F'. So I won't be wanting fish. Or fruit. Or French Fancies. Until at least next Friday."

By five o'clock he had told thirteen lies. Which wasn't a record. That was last Easter, when he managed to tell twenty-seven lies all by eleven in the morning. This time, however, Marcie had decided that enough was enough. Like Juju Jack, she was going to get her own back, big time. The question was, how?

Chapter 2

Revenge

Marcie would really have liked to stick Armitage in the washing machine and spin him on a hot wash until he was too dizzy to tell any more fibs.

Or make him rinse his mouth out with coal tar soap and car polish to clean up his act.

Or maybe dangle him upside-down in front of the lions at the Wildlife Park until he begged for mercy.

But the washing machine was too small, and besides, how would she persuade him to climb into it in the first place?

And there was no way he would drink coal tar soap or car polish if he wouldn't even eat fish.

And, last but not least, the lions were in bed with measles, and Marcie didn't think the penguins would have quite the same effect.

No, she needed something secret. Something sneaky.

In the end, it was Armitage himself who gave her 'The Brilliant Idea'. One day, he was in his bedroom mixing a strange potion of cough medicine and blueberry milkshake. The result was a slimy purple liquid that fizzed and smelled oddly of socks.

"What's that?" demanded Marcie.

"It's Anti-Fib Potion," replied Armitage. "It will make me immune to the lies of Juju Jack, the world's most menacing monkey, and his team of evil helpers."

Now, Marcie knew that what Armitage was mixing wasn't really Anti-Fib Potion. It was just fizzy, smelly, purple slime. Because Armitage was, of course, just a small boy with a big imagination.

But somewhere out in the real world were real scientists with real chemistry sets, who spent years mixing and testing real potions to make people better. Or worse. Or tell the truth.

All Marcie needed to do was to get hold of some, and fast. And she knew just how and where to do it.

Chapter 3
Dr Dullforce's New Improved Truth Drops

Marcie read every advertisement in the back of Granny's *Murder, Mystery and Suspense Monthly* magazine.

No, she did not want this.

A SECRET UNDERGROUND LAIR OF DOOM

Snap one up NOW!

Comes with its own moat, free crocodiles, and boiling oil! Full instructions included.

NIGHT goggles

All you'll see are stars!

MONSTER Munchies

Keep your Monster happy with these tasty treats.

TOP SECRET

The advertisement was quite small but it was exactly what Marcie was looking for: "Dr Dullforce's New Improved Truth Drops!" it read in bold, shouty lettering. Then, underneath, in smaller type, "Will root out little liars everywhere, or your money back! Super-speedy delivery guaranteed." And then, in very tiny type indeed, "Also good for tonsillitis. May cause spots. Do not operate heavy machinery after use."

Well, Armitage didn't have any heavy machinery. And Marcie thought spots would be a small price to pay for getting him to tell the truth. So she wrote her name and address neatly on the form. Then she popped it into an envelope with the £10 note Granny had given her to buy something useful. Which was exactly what she was doing.

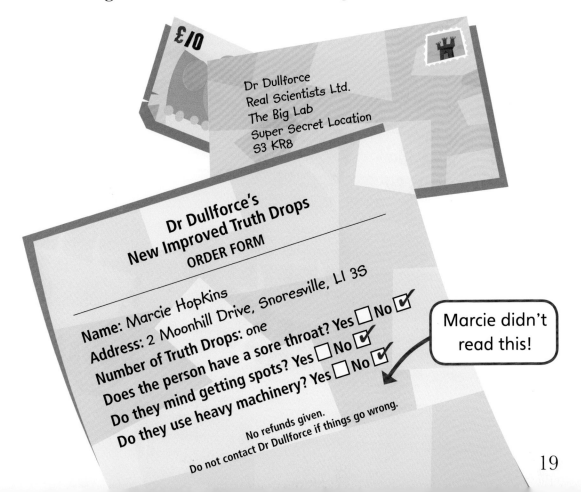

A small package arrived the very next day, which you must admit was super-speedy delivery. Marcie opened it and found a small glass bottle, with a dropper attached to the cap, wrapped in a sheet of instructions. Marcie read them carefully.

Put three drops on to the tongue of your suspect. Or, if working in secret, stir into their favourite food. Wait sixty seconds for best results.

Marcie opened the bottle and sniffed it carefully. Nothing. "Perfect," she thought. "I can put a few drops in Armitage's Crispy Cocoa Flaky Pops and he'll never suspect a thing." And that's exactly what she did.

Armitage loved chocolatey milk.

Marcie watched as Armitage slowly chewed and swallowed each mouthful of cereal. Then he put down his spoon.

"You've left some milk at the bottom," Marcie said, sounding worried.

"Oh, so I have," replied Armitage, and he picked up the bowl and drank the rest.

Normally, Marcie would have reported him to Mum immediately. But today was different. Because, any second now, Armitage was going to get exactly what was coming to him. Marcie watched the second hand of the clock on the kitchen wall tick slowly round.

Yes, any second now ...

Sixty seconds to be exact.

Chapter 4
The Truth

Marcie knew exactly what she was going to ask. On Armitage's wrist was a gigantic and rather horrid watch. It had three dials, and a little red light that flashed annoyingly every so often. It was the sort of gross plastic object that Armitage was very fond of. The sort that you save vouchers for, from the tops of biscuit packets. The sort that Armitage loved to lie about.

"Armitage," said Marcie, after sixty seconds were up, "where on earth did you get that horrid watch from?"

Armitage looked at the bulky piece of black plastic attached to his wrist.

"This?" he said.

Marcie nodded. This was it. It was truth time. She held her breath.

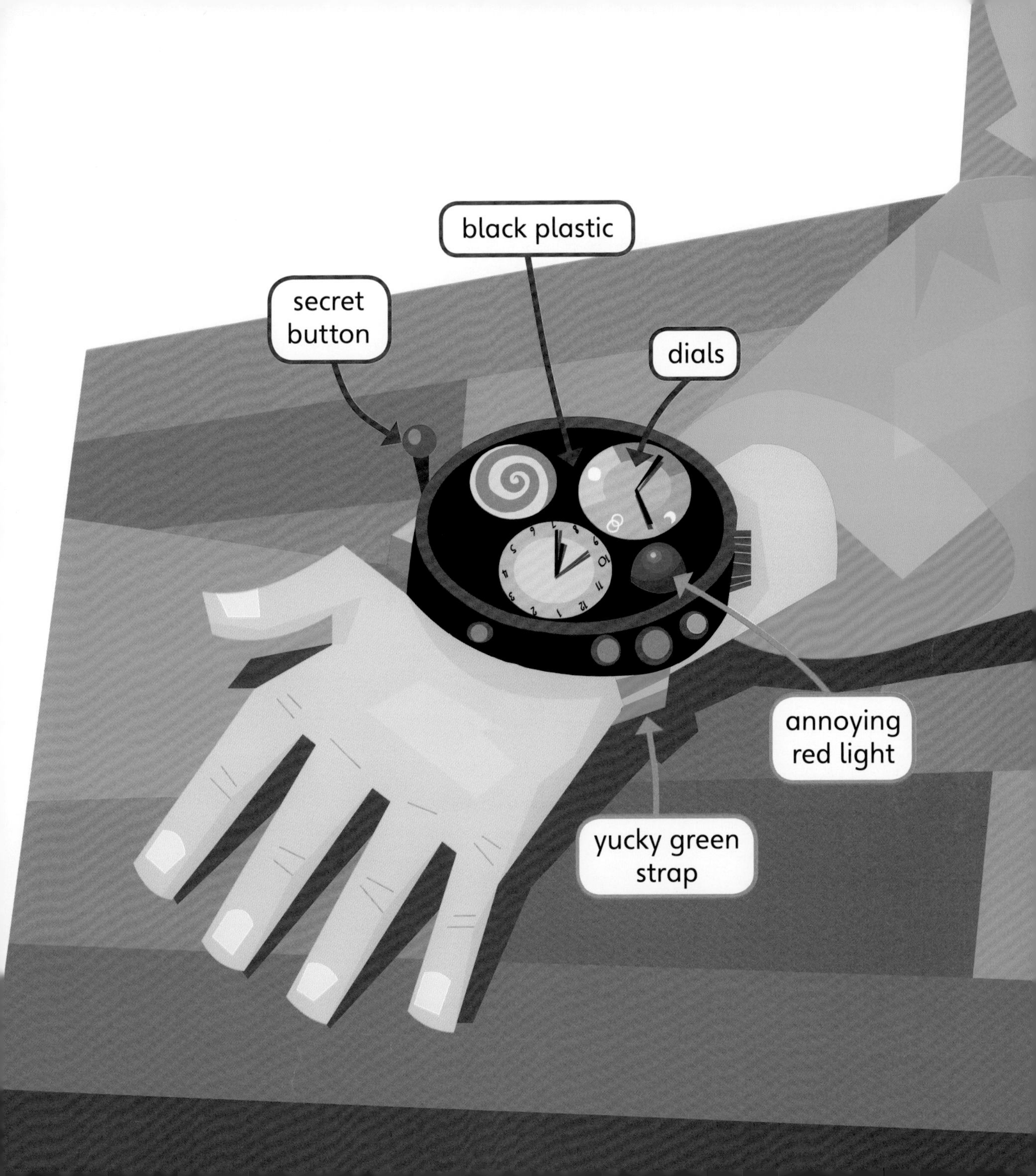
black plastic
secret button
dials
annoying red light
yucky green strap

Armitage looked up at her and smiled. "Oh, but this isn't a watch, Marcie. This is a Forcefield Generator. When I press a secret button, it sends out an anti-monkey magnetic wave that makes me completely invisible to Juju Jack."

Marcie didn't know what to say. "This is very odd," she thought. "Maybe I haven't waited long enough." She tried again. "Gosh. How interesting," she said. "And does Juju Jack live purely in that enormous imagination of yours?"

Armitage snorted and stood up. "Don't be silly, Marcie," he said, taking his bowl to the sink before heading for the door. "He lives on Planet Primate."

Marcie's mouth fell open. This couldn't be happening to her. She racked her brains, trying to come up with possible explanations. There were only two.

Number 1: The Truth Drops were a dud.

Number 2: Armitage had been telling the truth all along.

Well, she could forget number 2 immediately. There was no way Armitage was working for Lord Zarg, even if Lord Zarg did really exist. Which left number 1, that the Truth Drops were a dud.

Well, there was only one thing for it. Marcie would have to test them on someone else. But who exactly? Everyone else Marcie knew told the truth, the whole truth, and nothing but the truth. Didn't they?

Petunia

Barry

Granny

Mum

Marcie's friend

Chapter 5
The Whole Truth

First, Marcie tested the drops on Mum, who was in the
kitchen with Granny, playing Snap and eating Battenburg
cake. She put three drops in Mum's cup of tea and waited
sixty seconds.

Then she said, "Mum, is Snap your favourite card game?"
The answer, Marcie already knew, was "yes", as Mum
frequently told Granny that she liked nothing better than
a good game of Snap.

Mum looked up at Marcie and raised a single eyebrow. "Actually, dear, I can't stand Snap, but it's all that Granny knows how to play. And at least it stops her going on about her awful cat, Barry, and how wonderful Aunty Joan is."

Marcie gasped.

Mum clapped her hand over her mouth.

Granny said, "Goodness, I feel quite faint." And she picked up Mum's cup of tea and drained it in one gulp.

"No … Granny!" wailed Marcie.

But it was too late.

Exactly sixty seconds later, Granny turned to Mum with a very strange look in her eye. "And what, may I ask, is wrong with Aunty Joan? At least she can bake a cake that doesn't taste like wood shavings and sit in your stomach for several hours like a sack-load of cement."

Then Granny went white. "Oh my goodness," she said. "I don't know where that came from."

But Marcie knew. She ran out of the kitchen, out of the front door, and round to her best friend Petunia's house.

Marcie knocked loudly on Petunia's front door.

Petunia answered. "Oh, hi, Marcie. What's up?" But Marcie didn't have time to explain what was up. She only had time to squirt three of the Truth Drops straight into Petunia's mouth, which hung slightly open at the best of times.

"Yuk! What was that?" Petunia spluttered.

"Not now," replied Marcie, who was counting to sixty in her head.

"But …"

Marcie ignored her. "Fifty-eight, fifty-nine … right, that's it. Petunia, you know my best pink skirt that you borrowed for Casey Carson's birthday party?"

Petunia nodded.

"Well did you really post it back through my letterbox, only the dog must have eaten it before I could find it?"

Petunia pulled a face. "Don't be silly. I shrunk it in the hot wash on purpose after you won Pass-the-Parcel four times in a row and didn't even give me one of the Strawberry Sherbets you got as a prize. And now I'm using it as a doll's outfit for Baby Jane."

Marcie's best pink skirt!

"Oh," said Marcie.

"Oh," said Petunia, a look of horror spreading over her face.

Oh indeed. Because it seemed that Marcie was now getting the truth, the whole truth, and nothing but the truth from everyone. But now that she was getting the truth, she wasn't sure she wanted it. And the only person she had wanted the Truth Drops to work on was still telling lies!

What was wrong?

Perhaps … ?

Chapter 6
Nothing But The Truth

Marcie burst into Armitage's bedroom, where he was doing something with a pair of shoes that looked strangely like Jet-Action Rocket Boots. If those things actually existed.

"Have you taken Anti-Truth-Drops-Drops?"

Armitage looked at his sister. "Don't be silly. No one has invented them yet. Not even Lord Zarg. More's the pity."

Marcie slumped in an angry and gloomy heap on the bed. "Then there's only one other possible explanation," she snapped. "You must be immune."

"To what?" asked Armitage, pressing a red button on the side of one of the boots, and letting off a stream of worrying flames.

But Marcie was too cross to notice. "To 'Dr Dullforce's New Improved Truth Drops', obviously. I gave you some this morning, and here you are, still going on about Lord Zarg and that silly monkey. But when I tried it on Mum, who absolutely always tells the truth anyway, all sorts of awful things started to happen."

The wrong type of flames!

"There is another explanation," said Armitage, in a mysteriously quiet voice.

"What?" asked Marcie.

Armitage smiled. "That I've been telling the truth all along."

Marcie looked at the brown-haired boy, with the button nose, who was exactly like her. Ordinary in every way. Except one.

"There you go again," she sighed. "Really, Armitage. I do think that just for once you might be honest."

Armitage shrugged. "But I am being honest, Marcie."

Marcie got up. "If that's the way you want it, fine! I'd better go and sort out the mess with Mum and Granny downstairs."

"What mess, where?" said Armitage. But Marcie had already gone.

Marcie told Mum that the Battenburg cake was delicious. And she ate three slices just to prove it, even though it sat like a sack-load of cement in her stomach for several hours afterwards. But Marcie didn't notice that much. She was far too busy playing Snap with Granny, and letting her win every single one of the seventeen games. Granny talked happily about how Barry the cat could sniff out burglars at a hundred paces, and about the boogie-boarding holiday Aunty Joan had just been on.

Afterwards, Marcie went round to Petunia's house and apologised for not giving her any Strawberry Sherbets at Casey Carson's birthday party, and Petunia apologised for shrinking Marcie's pink skirt on purpose.

And Armitage?

Petunia loved Strawberry Sherbets.

He went back to making sure his Jet-Action Rocket Boots were working properly. Because Lord Zarg could call at any moment.

And he often did.